SOOTY'S
Adventures

ISBN 0 361 05469 6

Copyright © 1982 Sooty Concessions Limited
"The 'Sooty' Book Series" by arrangement with Harry and
Matthew Corbett. Approved by Sooty Concessions Limited
and Sooty Overseas Limited and licensed under Trade Mark
rights.
Published 1982 by Purnell Books
Made and printed in Great Britain by Purnell & Sons (Book
Production) Limited Paulton Bristol BS18 5LQ

Sooty's Steamroller

Sooty was mending the road in front of his house, and Sweep was helping him. It was dreadfully hard work, because they had to fill each hole with soil from Sooty's garden, and then bang it down with a spade. And it wasn't much better when they'd finished, because there were so many bumps and humps that it looked just like a switchback.

"What we want," said Sweep sadly, "is a steamroller."

Now Sweep didn't mean that, because he didn't for a moment think they could get one. So he was very surprised when Sooty suddenly dropped the spade on his foot and ran off down the road.

"Come on, Sweep," he shouted. "I've got an idea."

Sweep picked up his foot and hopped round in a circle. He didn't care twopence how many ideas Sooty had, he just wished he wouldn't drop

spades on his foot, because it was hurting him dreadfully. Sweep sat down in the road and counted his toes, just to make sure the spade hadn't cut any off. He felt better when he found they were all there though, and so he ran after Sooty, who was just disappearing over the little wooden bridge which led to TV Town.

You see, Sooty had seen a steamroller the day before, and Sweep was quite right. A steamroller was just exactly what they wanted.

It didn't take Sooty long to find it either, because it was parked right outside the Town Hall, where Mr. Bricks was mending the road. But Mr. Bricks had gone home to his dinner, so Sooty couldn't ask him if he could borrow it.

Sooty looked at the steamroller, and

he felt sure Mr. Bricks wouldn't mind lending it to him, and so he climbed up and poked his head inside the cab. It looked very simple too. And that's what he told Sweep when he came puffing up to him.

Well, Sweep didn't think it looked simple at all, but he didn't have a chance to say so, because just as he opened his mouth to speak Sooty started the engine.

Sweep clambered up beside Sooty, and in next to no time they were rolling along the High Street towards the little

wooden bridge. It was lovely riding down the High Street on a steamroller, and Sooty and Sweep smiled ever so happily as they rolled along. In fact, they had a very happy ride until they saw P.C. Nab directing the traffic at

the crossroads.

P.C. Nab frowned when he saw Sooty and Sweep on a steamroller, and he put up his hand to stop them. They did try very hard too, but I'm afraid they didn't know how to stop it.

Of course, Sooty didn't mean to run over the Policeman, but by the time he had found the brake and pulled it on they'd gone right over him, and he'd come out the other side.

P.C. Nab was as flat as a pancake. Oh dear, it did upset Sooty when he looked back and saw him. And of course he jumped straight down from the steamroller and went to help him. But before he had time to do anything Mr. Fusspot the Mayor came rushing up to them.

Mr. Fusspot was very annoyed when he saw P.C. Nab, and he said it wouldn't do at all.

"We've only got one Policeman in TV Town," he said, "and we can't have him going about like that."

Well, Sooty knew Mr. Fusspot was right, because it's not very nice to see a squashed Policeman directing the traffic, is it? But he didn't know what to do about it.

And I don't suppose he would have done anything if it hadn't been for Calico Joe. Calico Joe came riding along on his bicycle just then, and he laughed like anything when he saw P.C. Nab.

"You'd better blow him up again," he chuckled.

So that's exactly what Sooty did.

He borrowed the pump from Calico Joe's bicycle, and pumped up the Policeman. It took ever such a long

time to pump P.C. Nab up, but Sooty managed it in the end.

Everybody said he looked as good as new too, so Sooty thought he would be pleased. But he wasn't, you know. In fact, he was really quite nasty to Sooty.

Sooty was very hurt about it as he drove the steamroller down the road and over the little wooden bridge. But after all, as he said to Sweep, you can't please everyone, can you?

Harry Corbett's Car

Sooty and Sweep were going on a picnic with David and Peter. So Sooty and Sweep got up very early and cut the sandwiches, and they were all ready to go when Peter knocked on the door.

"We're ready," shouted Sooty as he opened the door.

But Peter wasn't ready, and neither was David.

"We can't come," said Peter glumly.

"We've got to clean Harry Corbett's car," explained David sadly. "He's going somewhere important this afternoon."

Sooty looked at the sandwiches, and Sweep licked one sadly, and then they both sat down and stared at David and Peter. They felt very disappointed about the picnic. In fact, they were so dreadfully disappointed that I think they would just have sat there and stared at each other all day if Sooty hadn't seen his Book of Spells lying on the windowsill.

"I know what I'll do," he shouted, when he saw it. "I'll magic it clean."

And he picked up the Book of Spells and ran out of the door, looking as pleased as could be with himself. But David and Peter weren't pleased, and even Sweep looked a tiny bit worried.

Now I don't know how much you know about Sooty's magic, but it's a very funny thing that lots of people think it isn't any good at all. I think he's very clever myself, but then he's never magicked anything for me. Anyway, David and Peter ran after him

as fast as they could go, and Sweep raced along behind them. They wanted to stop Sooty doing any magic, you see. But they were just too late, because as they rushed through the garage door Sooty had just finished saying a spell. It was a very good spell too, and if Harry Corbett hadn't left a packet of soapflakes in the car it would have worked perfectly.

You see, this is the spell:

Soapy flakes and bubbles too,
Give this car a good shampoo.

And that is exactly what happened. As soon as Sooty said "shampoo" the car started to bubble like a washtub, and in next to no time it was completely covered in soapy bubbles.

David and Peter were very pleased, because it would save them a lot of work, and Sweep was ever so proud of Sooty. So they would just have wiped the bubbles off and the car would have been as clean as a whistle, if it hadn't been for the packet of soapflakes.

But do you know, as soon as the magic reached the packet the soapflakes began to bubble like a cauldron, and before you could say "soapsuds" the car was full of them. My goodness, you've never seen so many bubbles in your life.

It quite frightened Sooty when he saw so many bubbles floating out of the car, and it wasn't very long before the air was so thick with them that he couldn't see the others at all.

He could hear them all right though, because they were all shouting at him to stop the magic. Sooty would have done so too but before he had time even to think of a spell the most terrible thing happened. The car rose from the ground and floated out of the garage.

Sooty felt very uncomfortable when the car floated away, but what upset him more than anything was when it stopped just above Harry Corbett's fishpond.

My goodness, it did frighten Sooty when he saw the car floating over the water. It frightened David and Peter too. And Sweep was so dreadfully afraid that he buried his head in the waterbutt.

And I'm glad he did, because that gave Sooty a wonderful idea.

"We'll hose it down," he shouted, and he ran and fetched the hosepipe.

Well, everybody thought that was a splendid idea, and they all stood and watched while Sooty fastened it to the water tap and aimed it at the car.

Whooooooooooosh! went the water, and it hit the car so hard that it shot it right across to the other side of the pond. It burst all the bubbles too, and

so the car dropped to the ground.

Sooty was very pleased when the car fell down, although it hit the ground with such a loud bang that he was sure Harry Corbett must have heard it in the house.

Anyway, Harry Corbett was very pleased with his car. He said it was beautifully clean, although he couldn't for the life of him understand how it had got to the other side of the fishpond.

And I'm afraid he never will understand that, because I'm quite sure that Sooty and Sweep won't tell him. And I don't suppose David and Peter will either. So don't *you* breathe a word, will you?

Mr. Fusspot's Ride

One day as Sooty drove his little car into TV Town he saw Mr. Fusspot the Mayor running down the road. Now Mr. Fusspot was rather fat, and he looked dreadfully hot, so Sooty stopped and asked him if he would like a lift.

"I'll take you in my car, Mr. Mayor," he said politely.

Mr. Fusspot beamed at him.

"That's very kind of you, Sooty," he said. "I was just going down to the Pier."

Sooty jumped out of his little car and ran round and opened the door for the Mayor. And then he climbed into the driving seat again and drove off towards the Pier. But he didn't get very far.

I expect you know how Sooty's

car works, don't you? It's a penny-in-the-slot car, and when Sooty puts a penny in, it goes; and when the penny runs out, it stops. So Sooty knew what was the matter at once, and he climbed out and felt in all his pockets. But do you know, he hadn't got a single penny on him anywhere.

He looked at Mr. Fusspot, but he didn't like to ask the Mayor for a penny, because he might think he was charging him for the ride. So there was only one thing that Sooty could do, and that was to magic his car to go.

Sooty took his magic wand from his pocket, and tapped the bonnet three times, and then he said a magic spell.

"Izzy, whizzy, fast and slow,
Magic, make my motor go."

Of course, Sooty ought to have got into the car before he said the spell, but he was in such a hurry that he didn't think of that. He wished he had afterwards though, because as soon as he said the spell the car shot off without him.

It did startle Sooty when his car roared off down the road with the Mayor. And Mr. Fusspot shouted so loudly you could hear him all over TV Town.

Sooty ran after the car like an express train, but he couldn't catch it. My goodness, he did run, but it wasn't a bit of good, because by the time he reached the bottom of the High Street the car was roaring up the Pier, with Mr. Fusspot the Mayor clutching his hat with one hand, and blowing the horn as loudly as he could with the other one.

Mr. Fusspot *was* making a noise, and everybody in TV Town ran out to see whatever was the matter. They all thought Sooty's car would go straight off the end of the Pier when they saw it travelling so fast. But it didn't do anything of the kind. It stopped dead right at the very end.

So everything would have been perfectly all right if only Mr. Fusspot had stopped too. But unfortunately he shot straight on when the car stopped, and plopped into the sea.

Everybody was very alarmed about the Mayor, and they all shouted at Sooty to do something at once. Sooty felt quite upset about it, because anybody would think he had pushed Mr. Fusspot into the water the way they were shouting at him.

Sooty *did* wish they'd be quiet, because he knew very well that P.C. Nab would come to see what was the

matter if they didn't stop making such a noise. And Sooty didn't want that to happen.

But he needn't have worried, because it was the Policeman's day off, and he was sitting peacefully on the other side of the Pier fishing. P.C. Nab was enjoying himself very much. In fact, he was very nearly asleep, when there was such a big tug on his fishing rod that it almost pulled him into the sea.

P.C. Nab beamed as he stood up and wound in the line. He had caught a big one this time, he was sure of that. And P.C. Nab was right, he had caught a big one. Because when at last the line came out of the water, Mr. Fusspot the Mayor was on the end of it.

P.C. Nab could hardly believe his eyes when he saw the Mayor, and he pulled him in as quickly as he could, and took the hook out of his trousers. He said he was very sorry too, but the Mayor didn't answer him. I don't think he could, because he was so full of water that a little fountain spurted out of his mouth every time he opened it.

P.C. Nab was dreadfully worried about the Mayor, and he went to fetch help at once. And the very first thing he saw when he ran round the end of the Pier was Sooty's car. So, of course, he gave Sooty a penny, and told him to take the Mayor home at once.

P.C. Nab felt very puzzled about it all. He sat on the end of the Pier and thought about it for a long time. But he couldn't make head nor tail of any of it. Mind you, I think he strongly suspected that Sooty had something to do with it.

Sooty's Fountain

One day when Sooty was digging in his garden he struck water. He didn't mean to, of course, because he was digging a patch for his potatoes.

Sooty could hardly believe his eyes when he saw the fountain, and he sat down and watched it soar into the sky. He felt very pleased about it really, because he had always wanted a fountain in his garden. And that's what

he told Sweep when he came out to see
what had happened.

Sooty and Sweep sat and watched the
fountain for a long time, and they felt
very happy as it sparkled up into the
sky. They wouldn't have been so
happy if they'd seen it coming down
though, because it was landing right in
the middle of TV Town.

Everybody thought it was raining at
first, and they all put their umbrellas

up. And I expect they would have gone on thinking it was raining for a long time if Calico Joe hadn't ridden past Sooty's house on his bicycle and seen the fountain in the garden.

Calico Joe put two and two together as soon as he saw the fountain, and he rode straight back into TV Town and told the Mayor.

Mr. Fusspot was furious when he heard about Sooty's fountain and he went to see him at once.

"How dare you make it rain on TV Town?" he shouted, as he ran into Sooty's garden.

Well, Sooty and Sweep didn't know it was raining in TV Town. And even if it was, Sooty didn't see that it was anything to do with them.

And then P.C. Nab came riding
down the garden on his bicycle.

"It's against the law!" he shouted, as
soon as he saw the fountain.

Mr. Fusspot smiled when he saw the
Policeman.

"That's right, Constable," he said.
"You'd better put them in gaol."

P.C. Nab beamed at Sooty and
Sweep when he heard that. He loved to

have somebody in gaol. And he was just taking his handcuffs out of his pocket when Calico Joe came rushing across the bridge with Mr. Plug the Plumber.

"It's the water!" he panted. "You'll have to stop it."

"It's flooding the town," puffed Mr. Plug.

Sooty and Sweep smiled when they heard that, because they knew very well Mr. Fusspot wouldn't send them to gaol if they promised to stop the fountain. So they told him they'd sit on it all day long to stop the water

So that's what they did. Only they didn't sit on it all day long, because as soon as Sooty sat on the water Mr. Plug saw a pipe in the hole, and then he knew where the fountain had come from. Sooty had broken a water pipe with his spade.

Well, of course, everything was quite simple once Mr. Plug had seen the pipe, because he just got out his tools and mended it. And in next to no time there wasn't a fountain in Sooty's garden at all.